W9-ABU-880

This Is Me, Laughing

This Is Me, Laughing

LYNEA BOWDISH

Pictures by
Walter Gaffney-Kessell

Farrar, Straus and Giroux
New York

Text copyright © 1996 by Lynea Bowdish
Illustrations copyright © 1996 by Walter Gaffney-Kessell
All rights reserved

Published simultaneously in Canada by HarperCollinsCanadaLtd
Color separations by Prestige Graphics, Inc.
Printed in the United States of America by Worzalla
First edition, 1996

Library of Congress Cataloging-in-Publication Data
Bowdish, Lynea.
This is me, laughing / Lynea Bowdish;
illustrated by Walter Gaffney-Kessell. — 1st ed.
p.   cm.
[1. Laughter—Fiction.] I. Gaffney-Kessell, Walter, ill. II. Title.
PZ7.B67194Th   1996   [Fic]—dc20   95-13860   CIP   AC

For my sister,
Edwina Sue Bowdish Henderson,
with love

L.B.

To Roses

W.G.K.

This is me.

This is me, laughing.
When I laugh, my whole body goes whoosh.

The laugh sweeps out
and dances all about the room.

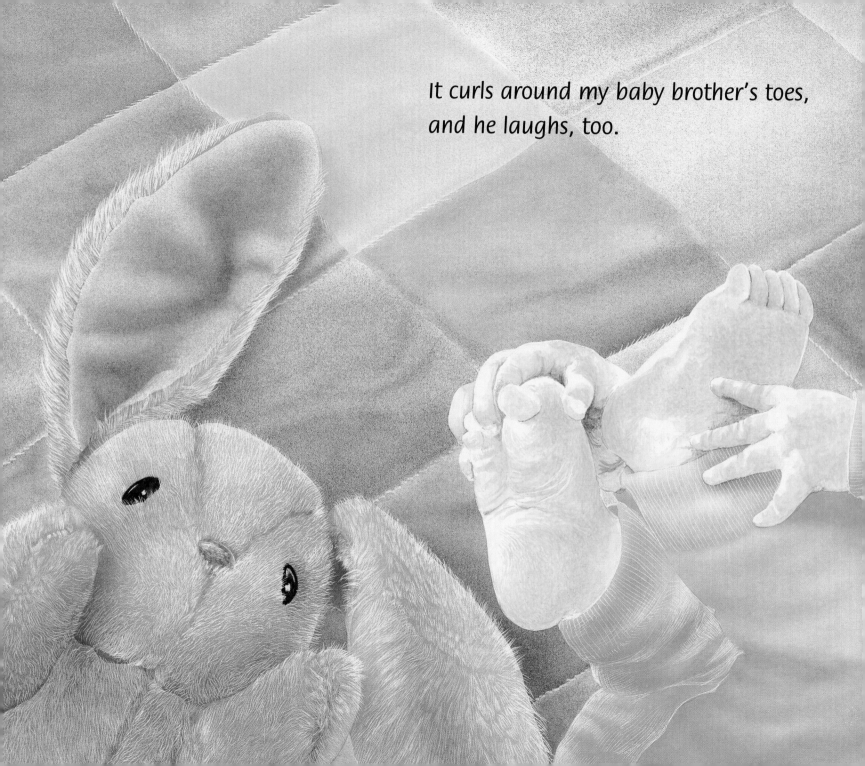

It curls around my baby brother's toes, and he laughs, too.

It rustles through the pages of my father's newspaper, and he laughs, too.

It catches in my mother's hair, and sparkles, and she laughs, too.

It wags in Chipper's tail, and flops his ears, and he laughs, too.

It rushes out the door and down the block.

It springs through Sammy's somersault,
and he laughs, too.

It tumbles through the mailman's letters,
and he laughs, too.

It circles Officer Reed, and bounces off her badge, and she laughs, too.

It twirls through Mrs. Prinn's petunias,
and tickles her gently,
and she laughs, too.

The laugh whirls up and down.
It turns around, and then comes spinning back to me.

This is me, laughing.